An Imprint of HarperCollins*Publishers*

Wagstaffe and the Life of Crime

"It's not us who should use our acrobatic skills," said Mrs Williams, "it's our one and only son. Old Clockwork Features. He's strong, he's fast, he's made of metal. He could go anywhere. Circus skills, my left foot! We've got a Human Cannonball!"

Mr Englebert Williams was staring at his wife in wonderment. If she hadn't been so ugly he'd have kissed her.

"Good gollykins, you're right!" he said. "We could train him up to make us rich! We could make him break into banks or stop security vans with his fists! He's bullet-proof! He's indestructible! Have another drink!"

Mrs Williams nodded. Her husband bought her a pint of best bitter and himself another champagne cocktail with a cherry. They clinked glasses.

"To Wagstaffe," they said. "And a Life of Crime!"

Also available in Lions

Split Second *Nick Baker*
The Crone *J. H. Brennan*
Elidor *Alan Garner*
Isaac Campion *Janni Howker*
The Nature of the Beast *Janni Howker*
When Hitler Stole Pink Rabbit *Judith Kerr*
Your Move, J. P. *Lois Lowry*
Wagstaffe the Wind-Up Boy *Jan Needle*
My Mate Shofiq *Jan Needle*
The Man with Eyes Like Windows *Gareth Owen*
Never Walk Alone *Gareth Owen*
Where the Quaggy Bends *Chris Powling*
Mercedes Ices *Philip Ridley*
A Free Man on Sunday *Fay Sampson*
Shapeshifter *Laurence Staig*
Death Knell *Nicholas Wilde*

Jan Needle

Wagstaffe
and the
Life of Crime

Lions
An Imprint of HarperCollinsPublishers

For David,
another Oldham wonderboy

First published in Great Britain in Lions 1992

Lions is an imprint of the Children's Division,
part of HarperCollins Publishers Ltd,
77/85 Fulham Palace Road, Hammersmith,
London W6 8JB

Copyright © 1992 Jan Needle

The author asserts the moral right to be
identified as the author of this work.

ISBN 0 00 674344–7

Printed and bound in Great Britain by
HarperCollins Manufacturing, Glasgow

Chapter One

Home Sweet Home

There's a song you'll have heard – if you like that kind of soft and boring garbage – that goes like this: It's very nice to go travelling (dum de dum), But it's oh so much nicer, Yes, it's oh so much nicer (bom bom), To come home. (Dah da). You know the one. It's rubbish, isn't it?

Believe it or not, though, Wagstaffe Williams's mum and dad were singing it in the back of the black taxi that was rumbling and rattling its way to their little terraced house in Oldham, Lancashire. Lustily, and loudly, and very out of tune.

Wagstaffe, looking through the bleary, rain-drenched glass at the bleary, rain-drenched streets, thought that they were barmy. He liked Oldham, fair enough, he liked to smell the glue factory and watch the dogs stop in the gutters for a cracking good cough before they crossed the cobbled roads. But then, he hadn't run off to America, had he? Unlike his parents, he hadn't thought it was very nice to go travelling in the first place. But for them, indeed, he'd never have left home.

Not only that, but he could imagine what the house would be like when they got there. Couldn't *they*, he wondered? Didn't they remember they'd flogged all the furniture before they'd abandoned their one and only darling boy? Didn't they remember the mice and the leaks and the smelly drains? Didn't they remember the bills they'd left unpaid?

(They did not know, but he did, that he'd lit the gas rings when he'd finally followed them to the good old USA. They did not know, but he did, that he'd rung the speaking clock in Australia and left the phone off, to run them up a mega-bill.)

Oddest of all, didn't they realise that they'd failed? That although for one brief glorious summer they'd been world famous acrobats and stunters with padded bras and long blonde hair (well, one of them) now they were nobodies? That the taxi-meter showed seventeen pounds sixty from the airport and they were stony-broke? Did they realise anything?

Whether or not (as they say in Oldham), Mr and Mrs Williams sang. Wilhelmina, a mousey lady of nearly twenty-five, who liked children very much (with HP sauce), and Englebert, whose wallet was so rarely opened it was a noted rest-home for old moths. They sang.

"It's very nice to go travelling (pom ti pom)
But it's oh so much nicer (la di da)
Yes, it's oh so much nicer (yes it is)
To come home."

The taxi driver drew up outside the house, pulled down his window, and spat into the lashing rain.

"Twenty pounds for cash," he said. "And I don't normally expect singing in the cab, so a tip would be in order."

Mr and Mrs Williams, who had trained as acrobats, of course, nipped nimbly onto the pavement.

"Cough up, son,' said Dad, flourishing his front door key. 'We know Mandy Badsox gave you plenty. I'll get your mother to put the kettle on. See if it suits her, ha ha ha!"

Wagstaffe, who was very, very rusty, was left alone. The driver glared at him, a fat white hand stuck out. Oh dear, thought Wagstaffe. What would Mandy think, if she could see him being bullied? She did not like pathetic people. She'd biff the driver for his nastiness, and she'd biff his parents, too. They were jolly now, but that could not last long. No way!

He paid the money with a horrible feeling deep inside him of disasters just around the corner. There was trouble coming, and it was coming soon. This time he'd have to face it on his own.

The driver slammed the taxi door, and the bang dislodged a loose slate that had been balanced on the roof gutter for sixteen years. Down it sailed, spinning gracefully, and smashed on Wagstaffe's head. For a moment he saw stars. That's typical, he thought. That's absolutely typical.

Home Sweet Home . . .

Chapter Two

Something Nasty

By the time Wagstaffe had squeaked his way through the puddles and the taxi had rattled off back towards Manchester, his mother and father had changed their tune, as he had known they would. No more Mr and Mrs Nice-guy.

In fact, as he hauled himself onto the doorstep, they were hurtling back down the passage like a pair of furies.

"Disaster!" shrieked his father. He was waving two fistfuls of bills, scattering them like confetti. "Destitution! The workhouse! Debtors' prison! Newgate!"

"The gas was on!" yelled his mum, tearing at her hair. "I picked up the telephone receiver off the table and it told me the time in Wagga-Wagga!"

"Final demands!" went Dad. "Writs! Threatening letters!"

"And where's all the furniture?" added Mum. "You naughty boy!"

Then she flung her arms around Wagstaffe's neck and squirted salt water all over his face and shoulders. He could feel it running down inside his shirt, adding to the rust.

"No chairs, no beds, no tables," she sobbed. "No

carpets, no settee, no cutlery. No curtains, no cups, no frying-pan. No kettle to put on!"

"No toilet-roll!" shouted Dad, from the lavatory. "I blame it all on you, Wagstaffe, all of it! We've lost everything. We haven't even got a clock."

"At the third stroke, it will be six forty-one and twenty seconds," said Mrs Williams, automatically. "In Ramsay St!"

Overcome with the horror of it all, she looked around her for somewhere cleanish to collapse on. Somewhere she could stretch out like an actress in a play, without getting mucky. But there was nothing except bare boards, covered in cockroaches and mouse dirt. The cockroaches were quite big and fierce, waggling their feelers.

"Oh Wagstaffe!" she howled. "What are you going to do?"

Mr Watkins Williams had emerged. He had only one handful of bills now, and a red face. He was looking rather cunning.

"He's going to pay," he said. "If it means no pocket money till he's forty-three." Suddenly a twisted smile broke out. "Look, you like pub meals, don't you?" he asked his son. "Fish fingers and chips, stuff like that? Cottage pie and new potatoes from a tin? Apple crumble with loads and loads of real synthetic cream? Lend us ten pounds, eh? We'll go out to the pub."

Wagstaffe, glad to be forgiven, fished out a note. His father snatched it.

"Ta," he said. "And while we're gone, tidy up the place, for heaven's sake! Ha ha, fooled you! I said *we*, not *you*! You should see your face!"

Two minutes later, they had closed the door behind them. Two minutes after that, Wagstaffe was in his bedroom, underneath the pile of coats that was his bed, trying to get some sleep. The mice were noisy, and the cockroaches tickled as they ran across his face and explored his ears and nostrils, but he knew he'd soon drop off. He was in a bad way. Exhausted. Finished. In urgent need of a doctor and an oil-can. He had to get attention very soon.

But he was still quite happy, strangely. He liked Oldham. He liked his home. You won't believe it, but he liked his mum and dad. It had been a funny couple of months, he mused dozily. It had been like a dream.

Was it a dream, or was it the plain, unvarnished truth? He really couldn't remember, any more.

Asleep, however, it all falls into place. Read on!

Chapter Three

The Story So Far

The plain, unvarnished truth is this: Wagstaffe Winstanley Watkins Williams is a Wind-Up Boy. His guts are made of clockwork, and he has a huge silver key in the middle of his back. He's a Wonder of Medical Science, there's even been a book about it.* This is how it happened.

ONE DAY, Wagstaffe's mother and father ran away from home because he was too horrible to live with, so they said. Wagstaffe would have disagreed, if they'd stayed to listen.

IN FACT, they'd gone to join a circus, anyway. They wanted to be Rich and Famous. They almost made it.

THE MORNING that they scarpered, Wagstaffe went to celebrate by playing on the motorway near Oldham. A lorry squashed him flat.

ENTER THE good doctor, Dr Dhondy. She kindly fixed him up with clockwork innards,

*Wagstaffe the Wind-Up Boy. It's a Lions paperback.

and surely saved his life. To show his gratitude, Wagstaffe spat in her eye and nicked a pound. Then he flew the Atlantic to America.

IN NEW YORK, he palled up with a wild girl called Mandy Badsox, who was stinking rich and lent him piles of money to get back home again. Also to get his insides fixed because he'd gone dead rusty rescuing his parents from one Theocritus Troutfish, Man of Evil. They'd been going over the Niagara Falls in a pedalo at the time.

In his sleep, Wagstaffe twitched, then laughed. Parents do such crazy things, don't they? He woke, and lay listening to the rain splashing through the roof onto the bare floorboards all around him. He sighed. They'd really had such an awful time of it, hadn't they? His poor mum, his poor old dad. World Class Failures, Total Laughing Stocks. He wished that he could help them, somehow.

And then it came to him – he could. He could help them out with some of Mandy's dosh, especially as he'd get his urgent treatment free on the good old British National Health. He could be wonderful to them, he could make things better, make up for their Broken Dreams. Mandy wouldn't mind if he spent a little on a really good cause, she'd wait to get it back.

Wagstaffe had a little glow of happiness. His mum and dad could be snappy sometimes, but underneath it all they loved him, he was sure. They knew how badly he needed an overhaul, how rusty he'd become, which is probably why they'd left him at home tonight, to get a rest. They were probably talking about him in the pub at this very moment, thinking about him, worrying about his future.

Smiling, Wagstaffe drifted back to sleep.

Chapter Four

The Brainwave

In a way, Wagstaffe was quite correct. In the Dog and Lamppost, munching scampi-in-the-basket and supping ale and champagne cocktails, Englebert and Wilhelmina were indeed thinking of their little lad. They were working out how best to do the dirty on him – fast.

"The Badsox cash is ours, of course," said Mrs Williams. "I mean, fancy that mindless trollop giving him the moolah when he can't count up to ten. We'll have to take it off him, naturally. For his own good."

"Yes," replied her husband. "Shut up a minute. Look at this, on telly."

It was that sort of pub. You could stuff your face and watch the box all at once. There was an item on about a smart new skyscraper in London.

"Ooh," said Mrs W. "It looks like an internal operation. All those pipes and things! What is it?"

"It's a building. It's the Floyds Tower in the City of London, where they make the cash. It's famous, it's won awards."

"Well, it still looks like an operation to me," said Mrs W. "It looks a bit like Wagstaffe, underneath his shirt."

The building was very, very strange. It was like a stump, made of mirror glass, with tubes and knobs and girders hung all over it. The lifts shot up the outside like bubbles you could see into.

"You've got no taste," said Englebert. "That always was your trouble. It's a masterpiece. Next, they're going to flood those great big tubes, see? It's going to be a building *and* a coloured fountain, the biggest in the world. It's going to squirt water hundreds of feet into the air over London, picked out with searchlights. The Queen's been asked to open it."

"Won't she get wet? Won't everyone get wet? It seems a daft idea to me."

Mr Williams flapped his scampi-basket to shut her up and hear the last bit, but he was too late. Another item flashed up, about a couple who had got away with a cool million at a Stately Home that afternoon and had not been caught yet. Wagstaffe's parents turned away, gloomily. They hated to see that other people were making money, however criminal they'd been. It reminded them that they were broke.

"That's what we ought to do," said Englebert, crunching up the last of his prawns in batter. "We ought to start a Life of Crime. Use our circus skills to carry out daring burglaries and robberies. I'll never get a proper job at my age, and you can't do *anything* that anyone would pay for."

Mrs W could have got humpy at the insult, but she didn't bother. She was used to her husband's charming little ways. She was thinking hard.

"It's not a bad idea," she said at last. "But it's

not us who should use our skills, it's our one and only son. Old Clockwork Features. He's strong, he's fast, he's made of metal. He could go anywhere. Circus skills my left foot! We've got a Human Cannonball!"

Mr Englebert Williams was staring at his wife in wonderment. If she hadn't been so ugly he'd have kissed her.

"Good gollykins, you're right!" he said. "We could train him up to make us rich! We could make him break into banks or stop security vans with his fists! He's bullet-proof! He's indestructible! Have another drink!"

Mrs Williams nodded. Her husband bought her a pint of best bitter and himself another champagne cocktail with a cherry. They clinked glasses.

"To Wagstaffe," they said. "And a Life of Crime!"

But first, of course, there was still the problem of Mandy's loot. They needed it, they wanted it, they *deserved* it. The only question was – how to get their claws on it? It took another seven drinks to work it out, and all the brainpower they had between them. Luckily, Mr Williams had been a teacher once, so he was brilliant. The answer, when it came to him, was simple, bold, and perfect.

Brute Force!

Chapter Five

The Deal

Brute force – but not on Wagstaffe. Because unlike most boys of his age, he was stronger than both his parents put together, despite his creaky joints. The first he knew about their plan was next morning, when he arose bright and early from his pile of putrid overcoats and fell headlong down the stairs.

Why? Because there weren't any. Outside his bedroom door there was a hole, with a few bits of splintered wood. All the way down to the hall.

"Yaroo!" shrieked Waggie, as he plummeted. "What's going on?"

"Grooogh!" he went, as he landed in a heap. Then, "Gor blimey strike a light!" as he stood up and put his leg right through where the hallway floor no longer was. "Holy Guacamole!"

"Language!" yelled his mother, from the kitchen. "Don't you bring your filthy American words to Oldham, you bad boy!"

Ignoring her, Wagstaffe swore on. The place was amazing. Clouds of dust and filth, holes in the walls, floorboards torn up everywhere. It was just like the Blitz(!). It took him five minutes of creeping and climbing to join his mum and dad. They were sitting on a pile of rubble in the kitchen, looking hungrily at the picture on an empty cornflakes packet.

"What happened?" asked Wagstaffe. "Have we been burgled? Has there been an earthquake?"

His mum and dad looked terrible. White-faced and bog-eyed with exhaustion. They had clearly had no sleep.

"It's your fault," said his father. "If you weren't such a mean swine, none of this need have happened. Where have you hidden it?"

Mrs Williams shushed her husband angrily.

"Shut up, slimeball," she snapped. "We're not going to ask him that, remember? We're going to play this craftily, aren't we? We're going to confuse him with our subtle brilliance. Leave it all to me."

She turned to her little son.

"Wagstaffe, we need money. Urgently. You're going to become a master criminal and rob banks for us. We're desperate."

Very crafty, eh? Dead subtle . . .

"What!" said Wagstaffe, totally astonished.

"You heard your mother!" replied his dad. "We're going to be like Mr and Mrs Fagin in *David Copperfield*, not that you've ever read a book by Henry Dickens, I'll be bound. We're going to wind you up and give you a small gun, perhaps, and you're going to make a fortune for us. We owe thousands, I haven't got a job, your mother's completely talentless, and it is – as I think I said – all your fault. So this time, Sonny Jim, you're going to do your bit. You're going to pull your weight. You're going to help."

His mother (thinking, perhaps, that they'd started on slightly the wrong foot) decided to play on Wagstaffe's sympathy. She burst into tears. They made white run-marks in her dirty face, and mingled with the droolings from her nose.

"Oh Waggie," she sobbed. "You've got to help us. We've been up all night. We've torn up all the floorboards, we've ruined everything. We're destitute, we haven't got a bean. We didn't even have enough to bring you a bottle of Coke and a bag of crisps back from the pub last night."

(What a liar, eh? It was Wagstaffe's ten pound note, as well.)

"Never mind," said Wagstaffe, "I wasn't really hungry, thanks. But why the floorboards? What did you do all night?"

"We were looking for change," she said pathetically. "Weren't we, Englebert? Sometimes you find small sums of money that have fallen out of people's pockets."

"Gosh!" said Wagstaffe. "You *must* be desperate! How much do you need?"

His mother and father both spoke at the same moment.

"Everything!" said Englebert.

"Not much!" said Wilhelmina.

"I still don't see why you pulled up the floorboards," said Wagstaffe. "That seems daft to me. Hang on a second, though. I was going to talk to you about this, anyway. Mandy's money. She'd want me to help you out with some of it, I know she would. I've had it in my hidey-hole."

Before their bulging eyes, he pulled his shirt up and bared his tin chest, once so bright and shiny. He pressed a button, and a metal pan sprang out. An odd smell filled the kitchen, something like the inside of a PE teacher's underpants. It was his dinner tray, that caught the food he stuffed down his gob. In a normal boy it would have been his colon. Perhaps a semi-colon, do you think? Wagstaffe pulled out something green and solid. A great big wad of notes.

"Here you are. It pongs a bit, but it's still good money." He picked and pulled at something else,

a little book that once might have been blue. "Oh blimey, here's my passport, too, I wondered where I'd put it. Silly me!"

Wagstaffe separated the greenbacks from the passport and tossed it to the kitchen floor. He didn't care much because it wasn't even really his, in fact.

"Ruined," he said. "It's a good job the money's all right. It's U.S. dollars, but the bank'll sort that out, won't they?"

On top of their pile of rubbish, his parents sat and gaped.

"For us?" breathed Wilhelmina. "Oh Waggie, that is kind!"

"Not all of it!" laughed Wagstaffe, feeling good, and noble, and generous, and content. "It isn't really ours, it's only borrowed, but a few hundred here and there won't be missed, I'm sure. I'll need a fair amount if Dr Dhondy's going to fit my extra parts, as well. She said she'd make me modern, more electric, if I ever had some cash. Don't worry, though, there's plenty there. There's forty thousand dollars."

22

Their eyes bulged further. Mr Williams licked his lips.

Wagstaffe said: "But no more of this crime rubbish, OK? No more trying to make me be a criminal. That's very, very silly of you, Mum and Dad, and I don't want to hear it again. Not a word. Is that agreed?"

Mrs Willie Williams skipped off the pile of broken floorboards like a mountain goat. She took the bundle of notes and pursed her lips. Wagstaffe pursed his, too, but it was the dollars she had in mind to kiss, stomach-slime and all. Ah well, thought Waggie.

She simpered at him.

"You're quite a nice boy, really," she said. "In a way it's our cash, as we're your parents and you're an only child, but let's not argue, shall we? We'll look after it, and we'll spend just what we have to and no more. Is *that* agreed?"

It was.

Chapter Six

The Road to Hell

It is possible (anything is possible) that Mrs W.W.W. Williams meant every word she said. Just spend a little here and there, be careful, look after all those dollars that were not *really* hers. Indeed, she kept to it for almost twenty minutes. Then – shortly after Wagstaffe had had his turn of looking at the cornflakes packet for breakfast, and wiped his mouth on his sleeve and burped – he went out to the hospital. And the door-bell rang. It was Mr Huddersfield★, the milkman.

"Good lord," he said, when he saw Mrs Williams standing there. "How nice to see you back home again after all this time. It's ninety-one pounds fifty pee you owe me, thanks very muchly, and there's a special offer on the yoghurt this week if you're interested?"

"Ninety-one pounds! How much milk did that little devil drink while we were away? Greedy Swine!"

"Tins of peaches mainly," said Mr Huddersfield. "And eggs for his catapult. He stopped taking cream after that Mad Cow Disease were invented. He said one was enough in any family."

★Try it without the aitch.

"Charming. Do you take dollars?"

"Do turtles mutate? I take anything. Phew! That wad smells like a pig's posterior! Here's your change, love – half a pint of silver-top and a cracked egg. Shall I start delivering again?"

At that moment a British Telecom van screeched to a halt. Three armed men leapt out, carrying a portable Japanese cash-register.

"Gotcha! If your name is Wilhelmina Winstanley Watkins Williams you owe us one thousand pounds and twenty seven pence. You've almost worn the Talking Clock out, but we'll let you off that if you like. You've got an honest face."

To their surprise and disappointment, Mrs Williams shelled out the dosh. They had no excuse for shooting anyone. As they went away the bailiffs turned up, in a lorry. They had iron bars and a Rottweiler, which was slavering so hard they'd tied a bucket underneath its chin. While it was looking for a baby it could savage, the bailiffs said they'd come to have the furniture, to a value of five hundred pounds for electricity, three hundred and seventeen for gas, seventy-six pence for stamps, and eleven thousand pounds and two pence for Trouble Caused when Wagstaffe had been doing mayhem. The Rottweiler was just about to take a lump of the local policeman (who'd cycled up) when Mrs Williams peeled off the notes and the bailiffs – absolutely gob-smacked – dragged it by its collar to the wagon and drove off. The bobby, Mr Anderton, was most impressed.

"By 'eck, Mrs W," he said, "you've struck it rich at last! That'll be with being a Famous Gribbleworm and whatnot, I shouldn't wonder? How about a donation to the Policeman's Ball? You'll be as rich as Lady Potter now, will you?"

A strange gleam came into Wagstaffe's mother's eye. A gleam of pride. Insanity, maybe. As rich as Lady Potter! It was like a dream!

"Richer, Constable," she said, grandly. "Far, far richer. Have a thousand dollars bill."

"Jimmy," said the policeman, not hearing properly.

"Jimmy, not Bill, Bill's my uncle. Thank you, ma'am. Delighted, I assure you!"

So eager was he to grip the note that he fell, smiling, from his bike. Mrs Wilhelmina Williams – still as grand as grand – turned on her heel and disappeared into the house.

As rich as Lady Potter! Oh, she *loved* it!

Good intentions, as the proverb puts it, pave the road to hell.

Chapter Seven

Three Things You Need To Know

Question One: Why did PC Anderton call Mrs Williams a Famous Gribbleworm?

Answer: Because that was the name she and Englebert used when they were circus stars.

Question Two: Who the hell is Lady Potter?

Answer: A rich and fancy old dame who lives near the Williamses. Very posh and probably broke underneath her snooty airs. What Oldham folk call "Fur coat and no knickers".

Question Three: If Mrs Williams was a Famous Gribbleworm, why isn't she as rich as PC Anderton thinks she is?

Answer: She and Englebert were conned by an evil circus-master called Troutfish, now no longer resident on this earth. He died owing them money. Two million, seven hundred and twenty-three dollars, to be precise. And forty-seven cents.

Question Four: Whose fault was it?

Answer: Wagstaffe's, of course.

Chapter Eight

A Boy and a Ferret

While Mrs Williams – her promises forgotten –
prepared to go and spend, spend, spend, Wagstaffe
was getting into trouble of a different kind.

It was a bus ride to the hospital for a normal
boy, but Waggie – to stop his rusty joints from
seizing up – decided he should peg it. Unfortunately
the Truant Officer heard his squeaks, and came
lumbering up behind him, wheezing and hissing
like a broken-down steam boiler.

"Come back!" he shouted, waving his black
book and cane. "I know you! You've tasted three
werms, you have! You've wissed meeks and leeks
of wessons! You're going to get a backed smottom
you are, ly mad!"

His false teeth popped out then (not surprisingly),
so Wagstaffe got away. Around the next corner,
though, he ran into an old friend, who was
looking very miffed indeed. In fact he was looking
ruddy furious.

"Waggie!" he spat. "I knew it were you, lad. I
heard you coming streets away. Where's my flaming
passport?"

The smile was wiped off Wagstaffe's face. It was
Hugh N'Dell, and he was serious. Even the ferret
on his shoulder, Danferoo, was frowning, as far as
ferrets can.

Normally, Wagstaffe would have escaped with
ease. He was a Wind-Up Boy, he could leap tall
buildings and bite the tops off tins of peaches. But
the ferret darted one way, and N'Dell jumped the
other, and Wagstaffe tried to trick them through
the middle. Quick as a flash Danferoo ran up
his trouser leg, holding him to ransom. He was
caught.

"Hi, Hughie," he said, lamely. "Nice to see you
after all this time. Why aren't you at school?"

"I were looking for you. The news you're back's
all over town. And I'm not called Hughie any more,

I'm Hugh. It's my new, cool image. I'm off to Germany next Tuesday."

Wagstaffe stared at his old friend, then goggled. The scruffiest boy in the school (except for him) was wearing clean clothes and a really groovy top! His hair was gelled! His teeth were hardly yellow, except around the edges! Was it *girls*?

"Is it girls?" he said. "What's gone on with you? Is it puberty or something terrible like that?"

"It's a bet," said Hugh N'Dell. "I've bet my dad a tenner I can act the Dead Smart Wally for three months. I'm off to Germany on a school trip next week. *And I haven't got a passport!*"

Omigosh, thought Wagstaffe. He had a vision of Hugh's passport, and it did not cheer him up. It was mangled, green and slimy, garnished with bits of chewed up bun and sausage. He'd done N'Dell a swap for it, when he'd needed it to get into the USA and N'Dell had needed Uncle Joe's Mint Balls.* He'd stashed it in his stomach tray with the loot. His mum had probably chucked it out by now.

"Oh yes," he said. "Your passport. I remember. Well, that's no trouble, mate, it's safe at home. Look, I'm in a hurry now, that's why I were running, I've got to . . . to see a . . . to see a man about a dog, you know. Look – call round this afternoon, OK? I'll give it to you then."

Hugh N'Dell was not convinced.

"I could get Danferoo to bite you," he said.

Waggie glanced at his jeans and laughed.

---

*They're sweets, made in Wigan, and they're fantastic.

"Wouldn't hurt, would it? He'd bust his little teeth, mate."

His friend could see his point. He called the ferret out, and put it down his own trousers.

"OK," he said. "This afternoon, all right? You wouldn't lie to me, would you, Wagstaffe?"

"Oh no," lied Wagstaffe. "I wouldn't let down an old mate. I'm just popping into town, then I'll be back this afternoon. No problems, honestly. I'm going . . . I've got to do some shopping."

Around the corner, looking like a heart attack on legs, came the Truant Officer.

"Ah!" he wheezed. "Bwo tirds with stone wone! Nou're yicked!"

But Hugh N'Dell had gone in one direction, and Wagstaffe in the other.

Wagstaffe was worrying. He hated lying to a friend.

But what could he do? He *had* to get to hospital.

Chapter Nine

The Price of Fame

Mr and Mrs Watkins Williams, when they went to town – Went To Town. In other words they Had a Ball, they Made a Splash, they Did Things Properly. When they had been famous for a while they had not been rich because their crooked boss had robbed them. Now they were rich they wanted fame again – and quickly got it. They spent so much money so very, very fast, that the newspapers, then the radio, then the TV got to hear of it. By the end of the morning they had bought up half of Oldham and were mobbed by men and women with ballpoint pens and cameras. They were hoarse from answering questions. They were delirious with pride. They were SUPERSTARS!

"But what have you *done*?" asked one confused reporter. "Mrs Williams, how did you *make* your money, tell me, *please*!"

Mrs Williams swelled with anger. What a common little man, she thought.

"Not Williams!" she shouted. "Gribbleworm, Gribbleworm, can't you understand good English, fool? Engie, darling, tell the common little man!"

Englebert said pompously: "We are the Famous Gribbleworms, fresh from our world tour. We have returned to our humble terraced home because we love it here. We are not stuck-up, like some!"

Most of the reporters, hearing this, guessed that they were bonkers, these two. Surely no one lived in Oldham if they could afford to live elsewhere? But as they followed them back towards their house, they began to change their minds. This was not a normal grotty street that they were going to. This was not a normal grotty house. Not any more it wasn't.

This was MONEY! This was CLASS!! This was AMAZING!!!

The confused reporter's eyes started to shine.

"Wow," he breathed, to his photographer. "Whoever they are, they must be loaded. Just look at all the stuff they've bought. We're talking *megabucks*."

Indeed, the scruffy cobbled street was in a state of ferment. It was crammed from end to end with vans and lorries. From every window of their house hung workmen, painting, repairing, rebuilding. As the world's press watched, carpets were delivered and laid – pink and pale brown, ivory and gold – curtains were hung and rehung by snooty ladies down from Harrogate, gas cookers were delivered,

installed, then thrown into the street as "far too common". A stream of car salesmen drove cars up to the door – BMWs and Jaguars and a white Rolls Royce – only to be told not to be silly, and to bring something better for the Gribbleworms to look at.

At first they paid with cash. But as their fame grew, as the TV cameras rolled, they did not need cash any more. They signed their names, carelessly, on any piece of paper held out to them. A thousand? Two thousand? Ten? A mere nothing, a spit in the ocean, we'll send your money in the post, we'll settle later. When people think you're loaded, they never check, they just *chuck* things at you.

By five o'clock, the Famous Gribbleworms were being filmed by BBC news, by ITN, and by seven local stations. They had given interviews to all the popular newspapers and to the *Guardian* and *The Times* as well. The line they took was very simple: the world-famous circus team had come back to their home town, their fortune made. In the crush Hugh N'Dell tried seven times to get to the front door to ask where Wagstaffe (and his passport) were. Seven times he was kicked into the gutter and trampled on.

And in a hotel room in Birkenhead, two people aged forty-seven, a dumpy black-haired man and a dumpy black-haired woman, watched the Famous Gribbleworms with great interest.

"I wonder if they're really rich," said the man, whose name was Simpson. "I very much doubt it, Cherry Pie."

"Me too," said Cherry Pie (whose real name was Mrs Simpson). "The last I heard they'd been robbed by Theocritus Troutfish, so they're probably desperate for a bob or two. All those expensive carpets!"

"They seem to be famous because they seem to be rich," mused her husband. "They seem to be rich because they seem to be famous. A conundrum."

"The price of fame," said Mrs Simpson, dumpily. "Or perhaps the fame of price . . ."*

"They know some tricks, though, don't they?

They were very good at tricks. My dearest, they could do the job, you know."

"Yes," said Cherry Pie. "They could do the job. When all the fuss has died down, when the TV cameramen have gone, perhaps we ought to get in touch."

The two dumpies smiled at each other.

"They might be desperate," said Mr Simpson. "They must have spent a fortune which they haven't got."

"They could do the job for us," said Cherry Pie . . .

---

*This is obviously absolutely meaningless, but none the worse for that.

Chapter Ten

Hospital

Being back in the hospital which had rebuilt him after his horrendous accident was very weird for Wagstaffe. He remembered it as being quite a quiet place, largely because he'd been unconscious most of the time. Now it was like Spaghetti Junction, hurry, scurry and bustle.

Two careless porters with a trolley drove right over him.

"Hey!" shouted Wagstaffe, from underneath the wheels. "What's the quickest way to Casualty?"

They laughed.

"Getting run over by a trolley!" they replied. "Shall we have another go?"

But they helped him to his feet quite kindly, and pointed down the corridor to a double door. Wagstaffe was limping now, his spring was nearly down and he felt very tired. In Casualty, which was crowded, hot and noisy, he spotted Dr Dhondy immediately, and was relieved. When she saw him, her face lit up.

"Wagstaffe!" she cried. "How lovely! How are you, child?"

Wagstaffe swayed. His eyes went blurry. He pressed a button, but his emergency batteries no longer worked, since their soaking at Niagara. As he collapsed, Dr Dhondy caught him expertly and whipped him into a cubicle.

Out of sight of the startled onlookers, she chucked him face downwards onto the trolley-bed and swiftly snapped out his key to wind him up. When she had finished she rolled him over and whipped his shirt up and his jeans down, despite his squawks.

"Shut up, idiot! I *made* all this!"

Then she began to Tut, and Hum, and Hah. Wagstaffe caught glimpses of her face, which did not reassure him. The Tuts and Hahs grew more and more frequent.

"Golly," she said, pulling up his trousers. "What a dreadful mess. What have you been doing, swimming? I told you never, *ever* to get wet."

"I drove a pedalo over Niagara Falls."

"Ho, very funny. Wagstaffe, you are a disgrace. You are a disgrace to the town, and to me, and to yourself. You have ruined everything."

"Me!" squeaked Wagstaffe. "Listen, *you* did all this! You gave me these stupid insides and this potty key in the back. What's more, you said it was only temporary. A botch-up job. You said when I came back you'd do it properly. Electronics! Bionics! Computer gear! Plastic instead of tin! You'd make me into a Proper Person, so my own mother wouldn't know me! Not a handless clock! So start! And get it right this time!"

Dr Dhondy, wearily, sat down on the pedal-bin and looked at him. Slowly, he stopped fizzing. Watching her face, he felt the start of fear.

"You are such a fool," she said. "You live in a

39

world of fantasy. I can't afford to think of luxury like that these days, we've been Improved. We have a waiting list five miles long. We use each bandage for eleven wounds at least. People share crutches. They take turns with the glass eye. How long have you been away? Too long, I fear."

She was sighing. She looked very sad.

"Look," she said, "if you could pay for it I'd fit you in and welcome, you could have a room, you might even get a bed. But as you can't pay . . ."

He was laughing at her. He was squeaking and rattling with mirth.

"Who said I couldn't pay?" he chortled. "Blimey, Dhondy, you're such a rotten miseryguts. Of course I'm going to pay. Just go to a telephone and ring my mum and dad. What do you take me for?

"A lunatic?" replied the doctor, wonderingly.

"Lunatic yourself. *I can pay*."

Poor Wagstaffe. Dr Dhondy was much nearer to the truth.

A lunatic . . .

Chapter Eleven

The Imposter

Ring-ring. Ring-ring.

An elegant hand picks up the telephone, all painted nails and diamond rings.

"Hellah. Gribbleworm Establishment heah. Madame Watkins Williams speakinah. It's the butlah's day orf."

"Hallo. It's the hospital. Dr Dhondy. We have your little boy with us. Wagstaffe. I'm afraid he needs an operation."

"Oh, reallah? How unpleasant for him. Will you let us know if he survives all right? Try The Dog and Lamppost, if we're not in. Lounge bar, naturallah."

"No no, you don't understand. It's a private operation. You'll have to pay. He says that will be all right."

A long silence. Mrs Watkins Williams, in a panic, notices the soggy pages of a passport peeping from a gold-plated litter bin.

"Oh! *What* name did you say? Wagstaffe? *Whose* little boy, exactly?"

While Dr Dhondy's mind was boggling, Willie Watkins Williams picked out the passport with the very, very tips of her polished plastic fingernails and glanced at it. She smiled, and chucked it back.

"You see," she went on, "we do not have a son called Wagstaffe. Our little lad's called Hugh N'Dell. And there's nothing at all wrong with him, I'm afraid. Good day."

Bang, went the receiver, in Dr Dhondy's ear. She glanced at Wagstaffe, smiling at her from the cubicle across the crowded room. What a shock the poor boy had in store.

Chapter Twelve

Englebert Has a Bawl

For all the talk of butlers, for all the gold-plated litter bins, for all the airs and graces, Mrs Williams and her husband were now utterly and completely and entirely stony broke. There was a pink Rolls Royce outside in the gutter, and two security guards (at thirty pounds an hour) keeping the local kids from scratching their names on it. In the kitchen there were two gas ranges, four electric hobs, seven microwaves – and no food. There was a chest freezer, a stand-up freezer, and a machine that could make enough ice to resink the Titanic *every seven minutes*. But there were no legs of lamb to freeze and no long drinks to freshen up with tinkling cubes. Mr Watkins Williams – when his wife returned from the telephone – was in tears.

"Oh stop blubbing, dear," she said. "It's all on credit. We'll think of a way to earn it before the bills arrive."

Her husband gave a whoop of despair. He pointed to a black plastic sack bulging underneath the kitchen table.

"They *have* arrived. The first six hundred. They're sending them by special messenger."

"How naice!" said Willie. "I hope you tip them

well, we have appearances to keep up, you know. How much have we got left of Mandy's money?"

He looked at her as if she were mad.

"Left?" repeated Engie. "Are you totally out of your pram? Mandy's money was forty thousand. Dollars, not even good old pounds. We've spent . . . we've spent . . ."

He scrabbled through the piles of paper until he found a scruffy envelope. He wiped his eyes, sneezed, then began to cry once more.

"I don't have to read it, I know it off by heart. I *can't* read it, I can't *bear* it. We've spent one hundred and eleven thousand pounds."

Mrs Williams got on her high horse.

"Well, I'm sure I haven't been extravagant," she said, flouncing her full-length mink dressing gown (a snip at twenty-one thousand pounds). "It must be you. You never did have any sense of value. You're just like Wagstaffe. He's in hospital, by the way, that was them on the phone. He's got to have an operation."

"More expense! I suppose he'll expect us to bring him grapes and comics! Well, he's got no chance!"

"Worse than that," laughed Wilhelmina. "He expected us to pay for it."

Englebert went pale.

"Good God. What did you say?"

"Never you mind. Just trust your clever little wifey. Would you like a nice cool glass of something?"

"Oh thank you. What have we got?"

"Ice."

★   ★   ★

Chapter Thirteen

The Coalshed

Wagstaffe would probably have been in tears as well, if Dr Dhondy had not removed his tear ducts when she'd done the original operation. She'd removed them in case the salt water damaged him. When she told him the news, he was so upset he couldn't even bluster.

"Hugh N'Dell? Their son? But he's a scruffy little jerk with a ferret. What's she talking about?"

Dr Dhondy was sympathetic.

"Perhaps she's under stress," she said. "Maybe it was some kind of little joke."

"My mum doesn't joke where cash is concerned," he muttered. "Money's not a joking matter to her. But it's not even *her* money! That's what hurts!"

"Surely it's not yours, though? You're not telling me you went to America and made your fortune? If that's the case, young man, you can give me back that pound you stole from my purse."

Wagstaffe, who was sitting on the trolley-bed, gave a laugh. But it didn't sound as if he meant it.

"Look, Doc," he replied. "No hard feelings, but I haven't got a cent. I did make my fortune, but like a fool I gave it to my mum and dad to look after for me. Like it or not, you're going to have to do the op for nowt. I'll pay you afterwards. After I've given Mum and Dad a piece of my mind. I can handle them. No danger."

But the doctor shook her head.

"No hard feelings yourself, but it's not possible. I've got half an hour break now, then I'm working till eight tomorrow morning. After breakfast I'm on sixteen hours more tomorrow, and the whole weekend. We've been Improved, I told you. They doubled the working hours when they sacked half the staff. Do you remember Aubrey?"

Wagstaffe did. A foul swine of a nasty ambulance driver who had wanted to chuck him in the pigbin before he was even dead; who had made Dr Dhondy's life a misery. He nodded.

"Well, he's in charge now. They made him Chairman of the Board because he said the doctors and the nurses were all overpaid and he'd keep us to the Spending Limits. One step out of line, Wagstaffe – and I'm finished. He hates me."

Wagstaffe Williams had never felt so miserable.

"But you've seen the state I'm in. I need mending, fast. I'm going to *die*, doctor."

Her big brown eyes were full of tears.

"Is there no way you can get money? We'd need five thousand pounds."

"My parents want me for a Life of Crime," he said. "They reckon I should make a million. I don't want to, it'll all go wrong."

"What do you mean, a Life of Crime?"

He told her, briefly. Dr Dhondy, an honest woman, grew very grave.

"No," she said, at last. "No, no, no. Not for

46

my little Wagstaffe, that would be terrible. Special people should *fight* crime, like Superman, like Batman, like that green bloke in New York. You cannot have a Life of Crime, I won't allow it."

"All very well," said Wagstaffe, "but what's the alternative?"

"I'll take you to the coalshed in the yard," said Dr Dhondy. "But *nobody* must see us."

Chapter Fourteen

N'Dell

And so it came to pass (as they say in Good Books, or one of them at least) that Our Hero, all tin and rust and squeaky-bits, was covered in a sheet that was too old and filthy to be used for even the poorest patients, popped into a wheelie-bin, and trundled out of Casualty's back door to the coalshed by the boilerhouse. Dr Dhondy had borrowed an overcoat from off a hook, and a pair of wellies from the mortuary, and a cap. She could have been a dustman, or anything like that. No one spotted her.

In the dark, smelling of coal and dampness, she found a filthy bench and helped Wagstaffe onto it. She gave him a torch and a copy of the Beano, and surprised him by bringing out a bowl of fruit from underneath her overcoat, to make him "feel at home". She didn't hang about, she immediately started unbolting this and twisting things off that, and pulling shafts and sprockets out of holes and crevices in his guts. Although there was practically no light she worked rapidly, and Wagstaffe's early panic slipped rapidly away – even when he opened his eyes and saw part of his insides being held above the doctor's head and looked at by torchlight.

"Crikey," he said. "This is a turn up, isn't it? How long will it take?"

Dr Dhondy was sweating.

"It can't take too long. Oh hell, Waggie, it's taken too long already! Look, I've got to get back to the wards! They'll murder me. Look, you go to sleep and don't worry, and I'll be back when I can."

"But you're on for the rest of the day! And all night!"

"I'll pop in. I'll get the stuff I need and I'll fix and oil and polish and adjust every time I get a moment. You'll be OK."

He was going to argue, but there was no point. He felt tired, weary. Run down, in fact.

"Oh well," he said.

"Good," said Dr Dhondy. "You're being brave. We'll be all right, lad, we'll have you on your feet in no time. Look, I've got to go. As long as no one gets to hear about you, we'll be champion. Just as long as no one knows you're here."

She left, and skipped in through the back door of the hospital, pulling off her cap and overcoat.

While in through the front door, his ferret on his shoulder, walked Hugh N'Dell.

It had taken him a lot of time to track his old mate down, and he was not going to be put off.

He was looking for his passport.

N'Dell

Chapter Fifteen

The Dumpies Arrive

Mr and Mrs Watkins Williams were having a screaming row when the doorbell went. It was about money.

"Haven't been extravagant?" screeched Mr Englebert. "Good golly, woman, those slippers alone must have cost a hundred pounds. They've got gold clips!"

Mrs Willie hit him.

"Two hundred, idiot! Who are you calling woman? And what about the Rolls?"

"I wanted to buy a Lada," lied Mr Watkins Williams. "I'm a teacher in real life, I know my value to society! Anyway, it cost another twelve thousand to get it painted pink! That was your idea!"

She hit him again.

"Liar! You said you wanted it to match your shirts! Anyway, why are you shouting? You started it!"

"What?"

The battering on the door had been going on for some time. They had not heard it until now. It stopped.

"What?"

They were getting confused. They were going round in circles. They had been drinking too much ice, maybe.

The hammering started up again.

Mrs W W said: "I think there's someone at the door. Oh, Engie, let's not argue, darling, everything should be wonderful. We're the Famous Gribbleworms."

"But we're broke! We're absolutely destitute! We'll go to prison!"

"But we've got skills! We can do Wondrous Tricks! We're Superstars! Are you *sure* that's not someone at the door?"

At that moment the door, tired of hanging around, fell off its hinges. Mr and Mrs Watkins Williams were quite startled.

"Help!" went Englebert. "It's burglars!"

"Take everything!" yelped Willie. "But do not harm my little boy!"

(So she *did* love him, after all! Hold on, he wasn't there. I give up.)

On the doormat (or rather on the door, as it was covering the mat) stood two people of forty-seven. They were black-haired and dumpy. The man politely held his hat in both hands across his stomach, while the lady was wearing a rather silly smile. She was holding a big bottle.

"How charming," said the man. "How lucky we are to find you in. The Famous Gribbleworms, the talented stars of international circus-hood. We'd like to offer you a little drink. Sweet Martini."

"How nice," said Willie. "It will go beautifully with the glasses."

"Indeed," replied the dumpy lady, scurrying across the door and onto the ivory and cream carpet, into which she sank almost to her knees. "We are so honoured to meet you. My name is Mrs Simpson. You may call me Gertie. What a lovely carpet!"

"What a lovely house!" said Mr Simpson "It must cost a *fortune* to keep up! And the Rolls! And everything!"

Suddenly Englebert burst into floods of tears. "And we haven't got a bean!" he sobbed. "All we've got is several tons of ice! We're in terrible, terrible, trouble!"

Mr and Mrs Simpson exchanged a quiet smile.

"We're millionaires," they said. "We've come to help you out . . ."

Chapter Sixteen

Go Ferret!

Hugh N'Dell, not knowing it was all a deadly secret and so on, walked up to the reception desk as bold as brass and asked to see his pal.

"What name?" asked the reception lady, kindly. (She hadn't seen Danferoo yet; he was up the back of N'Dell's coat.)

"Wagstaffe."

"Wagstaffe. First name?"

"Yeah."

"I beg your pardon?"

"Why?"

"What?"

Hugh N'Dell smiled his politest smile. Secretly he thought this dame was cracked. Adults and children often misunderstand each other like this. He thought she was cracked, and she thought he was a nasty little squirt. But she tried once more.

"We seem to be at cross purposes," she smiled, icily. "Let's start again. Name?"

He thought for a second, and made the wrong decision.

"N'Dell. That's me last name."

"Good! We're making progress!"

Writing it down, she said slowly: "Wagstaffe N'Dell."

"No! *My* name's N'Dell, his is Williams. Well, Watkins Williams, to be exact."

"*Whose* is?"

"*His* is! I'm called N'Dell, he's called Watkins Williams! Wagstaffe."

"Watkins Williams Wagstaffe?"

"No! Wagstaffe Watkins Williams. Winstanley, too. Somewhere. His mum and dad are mad."

It was clear from her face that the lady was getting mad, as well. Her make-up was beginning to crack.

"Oh gawd," said Hugh N'Dell. "I need to see him, desperate! Tinguts."

"How dare you!"

As she reached across the counter to give him a whang about the ear, the queue behind pushed forward to make it easier for her. At which Danferoo, squashed, popped his head out from the back of N'Dell's jacket (at the collar), and a lady behind him fainted with a shriek. As N'Dell turned round to look, the ferret and the receptionist came face to face. She fainted, too.

"Stop thief!" someone shouted (they always do) and a pickpocket near the telephones, thinking he'd been rumbled, stepped swiftly backwards looking innocent and knocked a patient off a trolley. The patient (who was unconscious) rolled into the goldfish pond and came round, roaring.

"Help help!" he yelled. "It's the Trojans! It's just like the Blitz!"(!)

An even older man, in a wheelchair, started striking about frantically with his rolled up *Daily*

Telegraph and thwacked a chubby nurse across the bottom (which he'd been wanting to do all day). She punched his nose (which she'd also been wanting to do all day), his daughter pulled the nurse's hair, and a porter called Cecil (who was in love with the nurse but didn't know how to say so) picked the daughter up and tossed her headfirst into the pool, where she swallowed two litres of water and a (small) carp.

Danferoo, assuming that all the humans had gone loopy, jumped from Hugh's head to a doctor's, from the doctor's to a taxi-driver's, and from the taxi-driver's to a nurse's. All three of them threw up their arms and screamed, while three other people tried to arrest N'Dell. A fire alarm went off.

Within minutes, the whole hospital was in uproar. Danferoo led, N'Dell followed, and a straggling crowd took up the rear, growing bigger all the time. They went from operating theatre to X-ray room, from maternity to geriatrics, from admin to accounts. Trolleys were let go down staircases, seven babies were handed to wrong mums (a cock-up that took eleven years to finally sort out) and fifteen

people had the wrong bits cut off or the right bits stitched on to the wrong parts of their bodies. It was chaos!

Hugh N'Dell, thinking he might be blamed for some of this, ducked into an office finally, which he was relieved to find was empty. He was sitting at the big leather-topped desk feeding Danferoo on bits of crisp from the inside of his pocket when the door burst open, and a most unpleasant man came in. He stared. From the corridors behind him came an amazing noise.

"Do you know what you've done?" he demanded. "Do you know my name? What's your name?"

Strangely enough, Hugh N'Dell did know this jerk. He'd seen him after Wagstaffe's accident, when he'd hung around to watch the fun.

"You're Audrey," he replied. "You drive an ambulance. You picked up my mate Wagstaffe."

"Aubrey!" roared the thin and twisted little man. "Not Audrey! And I'm the boss now, not a scummy driver!"

"Sorry," said Hugh. "No offence. I'm looking for him, as it happens. Now. Here. He's in your hospital somewhere. Can you tell me where?"

Aubrey's horrid face began to look much horrider. He was smiling!

"Wagstaffe? Here? In my hospital?" He let out a huge, maniacal laugh. "You, my boy, have signed his death warrant," he said. "You've done for him. Thank you."

Quick as a flash, he grabbed Hugh and his ferret by their scrawny necks, and locked them in a dusty wooden cupboard.

"Whoops," thought Hugh N'Dell.

Chapter Seventeen

The Suckers

"Ah," said Mr Englebert Williams, pompously. "But when is a millionaire not a millionaire? That is the question."

Mr Simpson popped another spoonful of Sweet Martini into his ice. He had an admiring expression on his face.

"What a clever chap you are, Gribbleworm," he gushed. "What a privilege to talk to you."

"You see," put in Willie, "we've been rich. We've been very rich. We've been very very *very* rich. We've been –"

"Dearest?" said her husband, with a gentle smile. "Please shut your stupid trap a second, love. OK?"

She went red.

"What we mean," she added rather snappily, "is that we will believe your millions when we see them. We Gribbleworms aren't daft, you know, and we do not come cheap."

The dumpy couple actually applauded.

"Bravo, bravo!" said Mrs Simpson. "Of course you have a price and we shall pay it. And of course you are cautious. You are right. You've known Troutfish, after all. Watch this."

To their surprise, she produced a video cassette

and put it on. To their greater surprise, it was a tape of the news, an old news. They'd seen it.

"We've seen it!" said Willie. "In the pub. After this bit about that funny building down in London, there's a bit about . . ."

She could not remember. She listened to the fellow droning on about the sudden snap decision to turn the outer tubing of the Floyds Tower into a coloured fountain. When the item ended, Mrs Simpson put the machine on Hold.

"About a robbery? In a Stately Home? An unknown couple who got away with a million in cash?"

The hazy outline of the hi-tech tower wobbled biliously before their eyes, all greens and blues and bulges. The memory flooded back. Yes, they thought. A huge, huge robbery.

"It was us," said Mr Simpson, gravely. "We are the mystery couple. And if you wait a second, we'll show you where the cash is hidden. We'll show you proof that we are millionaires. We'll tell you everything. Then will you trust us?"

Mr and Mrs Williams looked at each other, their eyes alight with stupidity and greed. They nodded.

"We will," they breathed. "We will."

Some people never learn.

Chapter Eighteen

Bad Timing

The story that the Simpsons told was simple, and in its way quite tragic. The dumpy little husband, pressing first the Rewind button then the Play, had teardrops in his eyes. As the Floyds Tower flashed into clarity on the screen, his voice was trembling.

"There," he said. "That cursed, cursed building. After the robbery, we went straight to London as we'd planned, and bought a tourist ticket to wander round and marvel at the architecture. We travelled up the atrium in the modular extra-mural elevator pod, and we explored the mysteries of the cantilevered tubes and fancy ductwork as laid out in the guidebook. In fact, of course, we knew far more than the guidebook told us, because we'd paid fifty quid a month ago to get a copy of the architect's blueprint. We'd already picked the spot."

"What spot?" asked Englebert. "The spot for what?"

"The spot to hide the loot," said Mrs Simpson. "We'd picked a nook, a lovely little cranny, that we could throw the bundles of money into without being seen. You know."

"How brilliant!" said Englebert. "So you posed

as tourists, carrying a bag? And at a pre-chosen site, you got rid of it! How wonderful!"

"What then, though?" asked Willie, who was slightly more suspicious than her husband. "What was to stop somebody else from finding it?"

Mrs Simpson tapped her lumpy nose.

"That's why we bought the blueprint. We'd worked it out to the last tiny detail. Exactly where it would be taken to in the ducting canals. Where the fans would blow it. What the action of the air-conditioning would do, day by day. Now, for instance. We know where the money is. To within a millimetre."

"Just there!" her husband cried, jabbing at the Hold button. "Inside that bendy bit. And by

61

tomorrow it will be at that corner there. And by the weekend . . ."

His voice tailed off, breaking with emotion, as they all stared at a weird metallic loop twelve storeys up, hanging giddily from the building like a coil of rogue spaghetti. Were they going to see a strong man weep? But Mrs Simpson carried on for him.

"And in two weeks time," she said, "when all the fuss and hoo-ha about the robbery had been forgotten, it was due to turn up in the street, at a Fire Hydrant. We'd be waiting, naturally, to collect it as it drifted past. It was so easy. So brilliant. So fantastic. And now it's ruined. We can't get to it."

"We need acrobats," said her husband, miserably. He blew his nose, hard, and perked up a little. "We need people with rubber limbs and wondrous skills. People of great courage. In short . . ." He paused, he smiled. "In short – we need you."

Mr Williams smiled also. Indeed, he thought, it did sound just like him. But his wife was frowning.

"But why?" she asked. "What went wrong?"

The dumpy man and wife became silent. The Mrs sighed, and the Mr switched off TV and video, and sat. He had a sigh to match his wife's.

"Friends," he said, "our timing was appalling. One hour after we hid the money, it was announced that the external pipework of the tower was to become a fountain. That's why our robbery only came second on the TV news that night, the Floyds news was even more sensational, they thought. The upshot is, that in a couple of days' time those tubes, that nice, safe hiding place, will be scoured by a million tons of coloured water, doing ninety miles an hour. The money will be shot from here to Kingdom Come, round corners, through grills, up pipes and down. If it ever emerges into the light of day, which I doubt, it will be lost forever. Torn to pieces, shredded, atomised. All of it. All four million. Gone."

The silence was broken by Willie's whistle. Englebert's mouth was hanging open slackly.

"Four million?" he said at last. "Did you say four? The telly news said one."

"The telly news was wrong," said Mr Simpson. "As it so often is. We got four million. Four million lovely smackeroos. Four million gorgeous greenies. *Four!*"

"And half of it is yours," said Mrs Simpson, briskly. "If you will go inside those pipes and root it out before the flood comes. If you'll track it down those nasty, bendy passages. If you have got the skill and courage. Half."

Mr Watkins Williams tried to stand but could not. His teeth were rattling audibly. His skin was white and sweating.

"But, but, but . . ." he mumbled.

Mrs Watkins Williams took him by the ear and jerked him lovingly to his feet.

"I'll get our coats," she said.

Chapter Nineteen

In the Apple Barrel

It did not take Hugh N'Dell long to get out of Aubrey's cupboard, and it was all thanks to his father, who had once bought him a book.

"Read that," he'd said. "It will take your mind off ferret-sexing for a while. There's a terrific bit about an apple barrel. I will ask questions."

The book was called *Treasure Island* and his father, a strange short tubby man with a beer belly, had reckoned it was the best book ever written. Naturally enough, Hugh never finished it.

He read about the apple barrel, though – he had to, didn't he? A boy called Hawkins hid in it and heard a plot to do the goodies in. After that, young N'Dell went back to ferret-sexing.

So how did it help him get out of Aubrey's cupboard?

Simple. After listening for twenty minutes, expecting to hear some pirates plotting things, he realised there were no pirates. So he broke the cupboard door open with his foot. The power of literature, see?

Outside, he loyally thought he'd better find and help his mate who could, he reckoned, be in a little trouble. What's more, he still wanted his passport.

But the place was crawling with security. He'd last five minutes. Less. Then it would be back to the cupboard, or the apple barrel, or even somewhere worse.

So he went home.

Chapter Twenty

Disasters Down the Line

When Aubrey finally ran Wagstaffe to ground in the coalshed, it set off a chain of disasters that echoed down the line.

The nurse and porter who had been helping Dr Dhondy got hit first and hardest. Nurse Sadie M'Gee, who had a special place in her heart for Waggie, tried to stop the evil ex-ambulance driver and his henchmen from getting through the door, ending up with a bloody nose for her pains. The porter, a curly-haired young man called David, sprang like a lion to her defence but was also beaten back and tossed behind the piles of coal. Other staff who came to watch got caught up in the fight, which spread from the coalshed across the car park, and into the admin block. Three cars and a wheelchair got overturned.

Dr Dhondy could have escaped, maybe, but she had not quite finished work on Wagstaffe. Her patient was still unconscious, although fully wound. There were a few connections unscrewed on his control panel, and she would have liked another hour, ideally. Some hopes.

When the men burst in, led (from behind) by the bold Aubrey, she did the only thing she could.

Gathering up Wagstaffe in her arms she leapt up a heap of nutty slack and carried on with the most vital jobs. When the men got too close she tossed furnace nuts at them and drove them back.

But it was soon over. Wagstaffe had been reactivated for only thirty seconds – he did not even know what was going on – when the doctor's arms were seized and she was dragged backwards down the sliding heap onto the floor. The patient was rudely grabbed as well, and the two of them were frogmarched through the swirling dust into the daylight. Shortly afterwards Wagstaffe – still in a blur – found himself in Aubrey's office, with Aubrey screeching and jumping up and down and carrying on because his prisoner – N'Dell – was gone.

By the time Wagstaffe could make some sense of the shouting, Aubrey had turned himself the colour of a plum. Even his closest helpers, his mega-creeps, were wishing he would cool it down a spot. Wagstaffe shook his head to clear away the last grey mists, and spoke.

"Listen, you slug," he said. "I don't know what you're on about, and I don't care. Where's my mate Dr Dhondy? I want to talk to her."

Aubrey's scrawny face twisted with hatred.

"Hah!" he went. "That friend, I'm glad to say, is dealt with. But where is the other one, the ferret-fancier? Tell me, or I'll call the police. The choice is yours."

Wagstaffe didn't have a clue where Hugh N'Dell was. But the choice was his. He took it.

With a surge of power from his newly-fettled spring, with every cog and sprocket spinning free, he leapt onto the desk and pulled Aubrey from his chair, bodily, by his ears. He tossed him in the air, reversed him like a rugby ball, and booted him across the room into the crowd of hangers-on. The whole lot of them crashed howling to the floor.

Then Wagstaffe bounded to the window frame, looked down for a clear run, and kicked the glass out. He threw himself into space, spun brilliantly round a flag pole, bounced from a corner of the wall, and dropped lightly on his feet outside the

main entrance. A small brown figure, leaving with a small brown case, came up to him.

"Ah, Wagstaffe," she said, ironically. "Full of the joys of spring, I see."

"Hi, Doc," said Wagstaffe. "Buy me a coffee, eh? I'm skint."

But she was skint as well. She had three pounds for the journey south, she told him, and she had the clothes she stood in. Oh – and she had the sack.

Chapter Twenty One

A Sort of Promise

"The journey south?" said Wagstaffe. "What do you mean?" Then, as the rest sank in: "The sack? But why?"

"Oh, don't ask silly questions, Wagstaffe. That's not the worst of it, that's just nothing. Look at this!"

Dr Dhondy fumbled in her pocket. She pulled out a crumpled piece of paper. Wagstaffe smoothed it out.

"It's a bill," she said. "It's what I owe them. Including VAT."

"Bandages, two pounds fifty," he read aloud. "Baling wire, seventy-eight pence. Lubricating oil and emery powder, four pounds eleven." He did a quick calculation. "But that only comes to eight pounds seven pee. Surely that won't break you?"

She gave him another piece, also with the Health Authority stamp on it. There was only one item.

"Use of hospital premises for performing private operation," read Wagstaffe. "Twenty-seven thousand pounds and thirty pence. But that's outrageous!"

She nodded.

"It's what we're up against," she said. "It's Aubrey Parkinson. I'm finished, child. Ruined."

Wagstaffe felt terrible. It was all his fault.

"Look," he said. "Doctor. I can't exactly pay your wages, but I'm sure I . . . I can get the money."

"Hah!" said Dr Dhondy. "How?"

Wagstaffe pondered. Even if his parents had been very careful with it, Mandy's money would not stretch that far. He swallowed, nervously.

"Like they suggested," he said. "My mum and dad. I'll do the Life of Crime. Yeah, that's it."

Her brown eyes flashed.

"No!" she said. "I would rather die in the gutter than see you do that, Wagstaffe. No, under no circumstances. *Not* a life of crime!"

Half an hour later, when they parted, she had made him sort of promise. He watched her get on the bus to Leeds, where she was going to find the Ml and hitch to London. Upstairs, in her raincoat, she looked very small and lonely.

He turned away in the cloud of blue diesel smoke, and mooched slowly towards his home.

He was going to have to have a serious talk with Mum and Dad . . .

Chapter Twenty Two

Wagstaffe Alone

When Wagstaffe had toddled off to hospital, you may recall, his house was full of cockroaches, and smashed up into the bargain through his parents' desperate search for dosh. It had changed so much when he returned, that he had to ask the neighbours if they recognised him, in case he'd come to the wrong street. They did.

"Aye, you're Wagstaffe," said one. "Best o'th' bunch, in my opinion. You can tell your dad from me, that if he parks that pink Rolls Royce outside my window when he comes back, I'll have the law on him. I'm sick to death of it."

Wagstaffe laughed, assuming it was a joke. Pink Rolls Royce! But it was true that the front door now had marble steps leading up to it, with a red carpet and a golden canopy, like at the Ritz. That was odd, especially for a red-brick terraced house in Oldham.

His key still fitted, though (not that he needed it, as the door was only propped up in the hole). And inside, he recognised the smell of home, even over the pong of brand new carpet. His eyes bulged as he looked around.

"Ruddy Nora! They must've won the pools!"

Even as he thought this, Wagstaffe guessed the truth. Pools be blowed. Mandy's money. He had been robbed. It was as plain as the nose on his mother's face, and that was *plain*.

"Mum!" he yelled. "Dad! Come here, you pair of thieving devils! Where are you hiding?"

There was nothing, not even any traffic noise. The windows had been double-glazed, the curtains were thick, rich, opulent. Wagstaffe ran from room to room, his ankles dragging through the carpet, his mouth opening like a fish's at every new wonder.

"Millions!" he breathed. "It must have cost millions! *Now* what have they been and done?"

He switched one of the giant TV sets on for company. A London scene, people queueing up with sleeping bags, crowds gathering in thousands for the grand ceremony at the Floyds Tower next day, desperate for a glimpse of Their Dear Queen. He saw a note, peeping out from underneath a bowl of fruit.

"Wagstaffe," (wrote his mother). "Wonderful houses like this don't grow on trees, you know, nor are they cheap. As you so viciously refused to help us out with a Life of Crime, we have had – as usual – to do the dirty work ourselves. However, if you think that you are going to share in the proceeds, think again. When we return we will be millionaires, and you will be Looking For A Flat. In the meantime, water the new plants, and No Parties. Don't bother to wonder where we are, because it is a secret no one knows. So long, sucker – start looking for that flat."

73

It was signed: "Your affectionate mother, Wilhelmina Gribbleworm (née Watkins Williams)" and there was one scrawled kiss. There was also a PS.

"PS" (it said) "Got you this time, haven't we? *Now* what are you going to do?"

Wagstaffe hardly had time to wonder before the doorbell went. It was Hugh N'Dell, and ferret.

Chapter Twenty Three

The Criminals

And where were they, his lovely mum and dad?
They were in a grotty doss-house, not far from the
Floyds Tower. They were poring over the blueprint,
and pouring whisky into glasses. Mrs Willie W
was already a Gribbleworm again, in her smartest
circus gear and a long blonde wig. Mr Williams was
smoking a small cigar, to make him feel tough.

"It's easy," said Mrs Simpson. "You go in Door A, down Corridor C, and into Manhole M. You proceed in a westerly direction until you reach Duct L, then turn south. Two hundred and twelve metres on you find Hatch H, and go to Tube Z. By the stopwatch, this will take one minute and thirteen seconds. End of Stage One. Perfect."

The TV was on in this room, also. A bald man with a spotted tie was telling the world how wonderful the day would be, how many people were going to watch the ceremony. Mr Simpson, with a calculator, was looking worried. Willie noticed.

"What's up, Mr Simpson?" she asked, her voice sounding rather hollow. "Is anything the matter?"

He laughed. He sounded even hollower.

"No, no! Everything's fine! Have another whisky, dear."

But he *was* worried. Things were going wrong. The time of the ceremony had been changed three times in two days, because the Queen couldn't make her mind up if she wanted to take official luncheon with the Lord Mayor, or have fish and chips at a nearby whelk stall that she knew. She also wanted to get to the local Oxfam shop to try and find a winter coat for Phillip.

Mr Simpson ran the figures through the calculator once more, but he already knew the worst. Their timing would be very tight indeed. In fact, there could easily be a disaster.

"There's just one thing," he said, very casually. "You know we're due to go into the building in the morning? About an hour before the Queen arrives?"

They nodded. Of course they did.

"Well," said Mr Simpson. "I think perhaps we ought to go earlier. Like tonight. Like soon. Like . . . very soon indeed."

Quite suddenly, Wilhelmina Gribbleworm felt a chill around her heart.

Chapter Twenty Four

On Yer Bike!

Mr Huddersfield, the milkman, was a tenacious sort
of chap. If you don't know what that means, and
you're too idle to look it up, I'll tell you. It means he
never let go when he'd got his teeth into something.
He was a British Bulldog. Although the Williamses
didn't owe him money any more, he knew that
something weird was going on, and he wanted to
get to the bottom of it.

Thus it was that he turned up at the smartest
terraced dump in Oldham not half an hour after
Hugh N'Dell. He was in time to stop the boys
from breaking *all* the furniture. They were having a fight.

It had started within seconds of Waggie's friend
arriving.

"You swine, Wagstaffe!" he'd shouted. "I've
missed me German trip! Miss says I'm too late!
I'll murder you!"

"You'll murder me?!" shrieked Wagstaffe. "I've
heard who gave me and Dr Dhondy away, you
stupid jerk" (Lies this, he'd heard no such thing)
"I'm going to lose my temper, lad!"

If he *had* lost his temper, who knows what might
have happened? He had the strength of ten these

days. But it was done more for enjoyment really, after the first punch or two, and they'd only destroyed three rooms or so when Mr Huddersfield appeared.

"Eh oop," said the old geezer. "Door were open, sort of. What's t'do?"

Wagstaffe, on the point of crowning his best pal with a colour TV set, paused. N'Dell, the dog, bounced a microwave oven off his skull.

"D'you know, Mr Huddersfield," said Waggie, blinking, "I don't really know. There's trouble coming somehow, that's obvious, so we thought we'd have a fight. Do *you* know what's happening?"

The old man smiled. There were whiskers in his nostrils, that waggled wetly.

"Aye," he said. "I've got a fair idea. Your mum and dad have spent thousands that they haven't got. Half a million, maybe. Tomorrow, Wagstaffe, the balloon goes up."

"But where are they? How can I do anything about it if I don't know where they are? They left a note but it tells me nothing. Where *are* they?"

The milkman waggled some more nostril-hair. He jiggled his eyebrows for good measure. It was a secret, see, and no one knew about it. Except him – he was a milkman, he knew everything. Over the next five minutes he told them of the mysterious dumpy couple, the dash to London in the pink Rolls Royce, and of something planned to happen at that Floyds Tower thing, where the Rich Swine worked.

"I don't know any details," he admitted. "Even someone as nosey as I am can't learn everything. But the Queen's doing summat there in the morning, and I'll put good money on it that it's all linked up. Mebbe they're planning to kidnap her and get the ransom. Your Ma will do anything to get her name in th'*Chron*."

"Kidnap the Queen!" said Hugh N'Dell. "What a laugh!"

"It's not funny!" snapped Wagstaffe. "Mr Huddersfield is right, she's publicity crazy. Look, we've got to get there, quick. We've got to stop 'em, whatever it is they're up to. Mr H. – lend us the train fare."

"Pass," said Mr H. "I've got two pound twenty-one till pay day. You could steal my milk float, though. I'll turn a blind eye."

"We?" said Hugh N'Dell. "Us? What do you mean, us? I'm not coming."

"Suit yourself," said Wagstaffe. "It'll be more fun than Germany, though. Have you got cash?"

"I've got a bike. It's got a –"

"Be serious! We can't bike to London!" Then Wagstaffe stopped. Great minds think alike. "It's got a what?"

"A dynamo. If you sat on the crossbar and I kept you wound up and we plugged your emergency battery into the dynamo, to keep it charged . . . I just thought . . ."

Wagstaffe's eyes were round.

"It's two hundred mile," said Mr Huddersfield. "But when I were a lad, I'd've done it, easy!"

It was the sort of challenge that Wagstaffe and N'Dell could not resist.

Even if – afterwards – they could not sit down for weeks.

Chapter Twenty Five

Night Work

There are several roads from Oldham to London and all of them – on a bicycle – are terrible. Wagstaffe and Hugh N'Dell (with Danferoo in a knapsack) chose the worst, because they thought it would be quietest. It was getting dark when they propped the front door securely up behind them, but it was not dark enough to guarantee a copper wouldn't stop them. Two boys (and a ferret) on a bike don't go down too well even with nice policemen, like Mr Anderton.

So they took the back road, the mountain road, to start with. They went from Oldham to Greenfield, then over the Isle of Skye road to Holmfirth. Which meant a huge long climb, five or six miles, with Wagstaffe sweating, and steaming, and groaning at the pedals, while Hughie kept his mainspring well in tension, and the dynamo pumped electricity up the cable that plugged into Waggie where a normal lad would sit.

At the top, along the flattish moorland road, things weren't so bad, then they had the wild, mad drop to Holmfirth, a nail-biter if ever there was one. But after that another long, tough climb before they neared the M1 at Barnsley, Junction 37.

It had taken them an hour and a quarter, and they were saddlesore and weary. Their first plan – to stay off the motorway – was quickly abandoned.

"It's illegal, and it's dangerous, and it's daft," said Hugh. "We'll not get five miles before we're stopped. We'll go to prison."

"And it's fast, and flat, and it goes right into London," Wagstaffe replied. "On the motorway I'll work her up to fifty or sixty miles an hour. If we see a cop car, we'll jump over the crash barrier and hide. If we take the normal roads we'll never do it. Wind me up."

They went.

Back in Oldham, back in the wonderful terraced house that looked just like a palace (inside) the phone was ringing. It was Mandy Badsox, wouldn't you just know it? When no one answered, she hung up.

And in London, three hours after midnight, Englebert and Wilhelmina, helped by the dark-haired Dumpies, sneaked past the snoring security guards into the Floyds Tower. They were wibbly, and nervous, and a little drunk – and as usual they were moaning.

"But you said we'd have a good night's kip," whined Englebert. "And you said you'd walk us through it. And you said you'd be with us until five minutes before the off!"

"Well we can't be," snarled Mrs Simpson. "You've got to do it on your own. It's so easy, anyway! At eleven fifteen precisely, you put the stuff into the side duct, like we told you. The water pressure will do the rest."

"But where will you be?"

"Waiting to get you out, of course. What do you take us for? We've got to save the situation, ours is the hard part of the job. You follow your instructions, and we'll see you at midday. Everything in the garden will be lovely, and we'll all be rich. Just don't moan!"

The Williamses – or the Famous Gribbleworms, they were both in costume now – were pushed, still moaning, into Manhole M, which the Dumpies locked behind them. When the high, querulous voices were muffled at last by good thick steel, the couple mopped their brows.

"We're doing the world a favour, if you ask me," said Mrs Simpson. "What a pair of whingers!"

"Yes," said her husband. He mimicked them: "But where will *you* be?"

His wife laughed, evilly.

"Waiting at Fire Hydrant P, in Sackville Street, for the cash to pop out," she said. "While you, my dear Gribbleworms – are minced into blobs of rosy froth, another colour for the lovely coloured fountain. With teeth and eyebrows thrown in."

Her husband took her elbow as they headed for the door.

"And won't that be a dainty dish to set before the Queen!"

Chapter Twenty Six

Royal Progress

If Wagstaffe and N'Dell really thought they could go from Oldham to London on a motorway by bike and not be noticed by the Men in Blue they were raving. By the time they passed Birmingham three motorists had driven off the road while trying to get a better view of them, and at Derby a clergyman in a Morris Minor did a U-turn across all three lanes and caused a tailback twelve miles long. But however hard the police looked, they failed to find the boys. They were on a bike, they had no lights, and Wagstaffe was punching them along at up to sixty. Several motorists were arrested on suspicion of being drunk because of the description that they gave. Meanwhile – our heroes thundered on.

But in London, all that stopped. Wagstaffe and N'Dell, having rested in a haystack for the longest, darkest part of night, reached the end of the motorway in the morning rush hour. Their speed went from Fast to Very Slow. The Men in Blue caught up.

It's a sad fact about London that traffic moves at a sticky, smoky crawl. In the 1920s, when petrol taxis took over from the horse-drawn cabs, they could average twelve miles an hour – very fast, they thought. In the 1990s taxis (and everybody else) can only manage eight. So every time they saw a policeman, or vice versa, our boys were chased. First by flatfoots, then by Nods with pedal-power, then by motor-bike patrols. Cars, of course, were useless, although there was the police helicopter to contend with. By ten o'clock – lost, exhausted and starving – they were getting desperate. And they had no idea exactly which way they should be heading.

It was a traffic jam that saved them. A mega, minta, monster, top-ace snarl up. Gradually they realised, as they ducked and wove along pavements and down back alleys, always just one jump ahead of all the chasers, that this one was Something Special. People were beginning to get out of their cars and switch off their engines. Lorry drivers were climb-

ing onto their cabs to look ahead, and passengers were abandoning their buses. As Wagstaffe and N'Dell pushed deeper into the heart of it, they noticed Union Jacks. They were being waved by little children in their Sunday best standing on the pavements. They were fluttering from flagpoles on tall buildings. They were hanging out of upstairs windows. Up ahead there was a barrier across the road, and it was festooned with them, red, white and blue. At the barrier, the traffic stopped. Beyond it there were only people, waiting.

"It's the route!" said Hugh N'Dell, into Waggie's earhole. "It's the way the Queen's to go, to get to Floyds! Get past it, lad!"

Wagstaffe put on an enormous spurt and the barrier rushed towards them. The police all round it

looked amazed, then horrified, as the bike screamed across the tarmac, smoke pouring from its tyres. At the last moment the two boys ducked, and the coppers jumped at them. They missed. They shouted. They blew whistles. Wagstaffe, clear, braked like mad, before he hit the crowds.

And miraculously, the crowds parted. Ahead of them, a huge cheer rose up, a sea of Union Jacks began to wave. As Wagstaffe and N'Dell rode along, the rumour spread before them – it's the Queen, the Queen, the Queen! And to applause and laughter, they pedalled gently the last two miles into the square, into the shadow of the strange, tall building that reminded Wagstaffe of a Lego fantasy covered in intestines. Behind them, as they rode, the crowds closed in again, pleased at their mistake in thinking this was Royalty – and blocking off the following police completely. In the mighty, pulsing mass thronging the Square, the boys from Oldham were alone upon their bike.

Except that when they stopped it, wondering what the heck they were going to do now – they came face to face with Mr and Mrs Simpson, smiling in the sunshine as if the Floyds Tower were their own personal piggy bank, about to make a pay-out. Which, in a way, it was.

It was one of those coincidences that could only happen in a book. Lucky, eh? And Hugh and Wagstaffe – who had been given good descriptions of the Simpsons by Mr Huddersfield ("Short, dumpy, black-haired, forty-seven") – recognised them immediately. "Here!" said Wagstaffe, leaping off the bike. "We want a word with you!"

Chapter Twenty Seven

In the Apple Barrel (Again)

Mr and Mrs Simpson could have run. They could have disappeared into the crowd never to be seen again. They could have even (if they'd had one) drawn a gun. They chose, instead, to play it crafty.

"Ah! Wagstaffe!" said Mrs Simpson (who was the clever one) "Your parents said we'd find you here! You *are* Wagstaffe, aren't you, lad? We've seen the photographs."

In view of the fact that Wagstaffe, all hot and bothered, was sweating gobs of oil and his key was poking through the slit in the back of his jacket, it wasn't too difficult as a guess. But their boldness confused him.

"Yes," he replied, "I'm Wagstaffe. But you're the villains, why are you smiling? You've kidnapped Mum and Dad!"

Mr Simpson roared with laughter. He'd caught on fast.

"Kidnapped them? They're our friends! Do you want to see them? Have a word?"

Indeed he did! And the Dumpies did not give him time to think it through. As in a whirlwind, the two lads were hurried through the crowds. Like two young dumbclucks they gaped at the stinking entrance to the doss-house they were taken to (chaining the bike to the railings outside). Like a pair of gawping kids they went up in the rickety old lift and waited while Mr Simpson opened up the paint-peeling door.

"Where are they, then?" asked Wagstaffe, going in. "Mum! Dad!"

The Simpsons fell about. Mrs closed the door.

"Children!" she chortled. "They're so stupid! It's like taking sweeties off a blind man!"

"What?" said Wagstaffe. "What are you on about? You said that they were here!"

"But they're not, are they? They're not here, little fool, because they're in the pipework of the Floyds Tower, looking for our loot. And in ten minutes time or so – when the Queen gets here to press the button – they're going to be dead meat!"

She looked such a normal person, did Mrs Simpson, that Wagstaffe did not believe her.

"You what?" was all he said.

"You heard!" replied the normal-looking husband. "When the Queen presses the switch the pumps start up, OK? The coloured water thunders through the pipes, pushing everything before it, including your parents and all our cash. For two minutes it goes round and round the system, until the whole network of pipes is at full pressure. Then – automatically – the next stage starts. Valves open, another switch cuts in. And all that power, enough to knock the Eiffel Tower flat, is squirted upwards through a hole no bigger than a two-pee piece. A coloured fountain right across the sky."

Now Wagstaffe knew that they were kidding him.

"But if your money's squirted through a tiny hole, what use will it be?" he said. "That's stupid."

"Oh no it's not," said Mrs Simpson. "That's where your Ma and Pa come in. They'll have placed the money in a special duct, that's their job. There's a network of escape tubes, to relieve the pressure. The second stage will blow our money straight down this network to Fire Hydrant P, in Sackville Street. Where we will be waiting with our little plastic bag to collect it. Neat, eh?"

"And Mum and Dad?" asked Wagstaffe, coldly. "How big is Hydrant P?"

The dumpy lady tittered.

"Oh no," she said. "They, I'm afraid, go the other way. Through the two-pee piece. They'll come to earth as a nice pink spray. Let's hope our dear Monarch has brought her umbrella."

"Go!" yelled Hugh N'Dell, and launched himself at Mrs Simpson, who hit him a great clout upon the bonce with her handbag. In which, it would appear, she carried half a brick. Wagstaffe fared no better, as Mr Simpson neatly tripped him up and smothered him in a bedspread, his arms and legs a total tangle. Only Danferoo escaped, leaping from Hughie's shoulders, running up a curtain, and disappearing.

Two minutes later the boys were locked in a wardrobe, a very stout one.

The Dumpies – cackling – had gone.

Chapter Twenty Eight

The Bowels of the Beast

In the bowels of the beast (or inside the Floyds Tower ducting system, at least) Mrs Wilhelmina Watkins Williams and her faithful Englebert were beginning to realise a little of what was going on.

"These passages are too narrow for human beings," said Willie. "My tutu is all squashed. My tights are laddered."

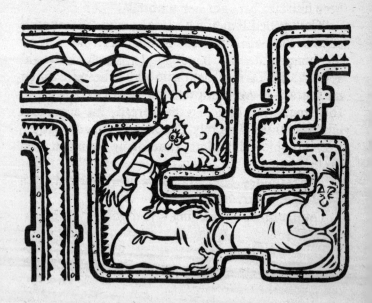

(They had done the job. They had done Door A, and Corridor C and Tube Z, and so on. They had shifted the bundles of cash from one spot to another, all was very well.)

"It's getting hot," said Englebert. "The puffs of steam are curling my moustachio."

(They were in full circus gear – the leotards, the false moustaches, all the sequins.)

"Those noises down the passageways," said Wilhelmina. "They sound like something's boiling, like there's an explosion brewing. Englebert – I want to get out now."

(Mr Watkins Williams had reached a crossroads in the piping. There were three routes to choose from and all of them looked terrible. The steam from the boilers was increasing. The time was very, very close.)

"Courage, my pet!" he said, gaily. "When this is over we will laugh at the memory! We will be laughing millionaires!"

And suddenly, in the throbbing, hissing, boiling passageways, they both felt hot water gushing down their faces.

It was their tears . . .

Chapter Twenty Nine

Just A Minute

By the time Wagstaffe and Hugh N'Dell escaped (and they did, of course, they did) Willie and Englebert were probably past saving. The Queen had driven through the mighty crowds in her open car, waving at her loyal subjects and smiling her fixed smile, and the Guard of Honour had presented arms at the steps to the platform where she was to press the button.

Her courtiers – smarmy men in suits and floral-hatted women with blue hair – had scurried hither and thither smirking, and the gentleman from ITN had kissed the ground eleven times in front of her in the hope that she might knight him on the spot. Flowers were thrown, women fainted, the cheers swelled so loudly they drowned the noise of jetplanes overhead.

In the wardrobe Hugh and Wagstaffe had been fighting, and they still weren't the best of friends. N'Dell (who'd gone a little funny from the brick) had spent ages wittering about apple barrels and hidden treasure, until Wagstaffe – exasperated – had kicked the door out with his metal heel to get away from it. Then his mate had wittered on about his ferret (which had gone missing) and his bicycle, which had gone missing, too. (Only the wheel was left, chained to the railings. They were in London, after all.)

"Shut up!" shouted Wagstaffe, on the pavement. "I don't care about Danferoo! I don't care about your rotten bike! What about my rotten parents?"

At that moment they heard a gigantic roar. Then a chant, two streets away: "The Queen! The Queen!"

"Oh gawd," said Wagstaffe. "Listen, mate, this is no time for quarrelling. Get to Sackville Street, *please*. Fire Hydrant P. Find that pair of little tubby gets and stop them. I'll buy you a new one! Twenty-seven gears!"

Hugh N'Dell was gone. He shot off like a bullet from a gun. Wagstaffe watched him reach the crowd and burrow into it like a maggot through a plum. There were people everywhere, filling every street, far too far away to get their eyeballs on the Queen. Another cheer spread from the centre.

Then, with a crackle and a buzz, a cultured lady's voice came booming through loudspeakers. So that was it. If you could not see you'd listen. The splendid accent filled the air.

"Dear friends," the Queen said. "My loyal subjects, from the highest of you to the veriest unwashed scum that hang around street corners. We are gathered here today to honour the men and women whose greed and lust for easy money have put the greatness back into our dear Great Britain, the folks of Floyds. The task we are about to perform, the pressing of this little switch in sixty seconds time, is a symbolic one. In fact, it's a lot of symbols, and a load of –"

Wagstaffe was no longer listening. He was running, running, running at the crowd. He was pushing, shoving, kicking, biting, growling to get through.

The Queen was about to press the button. His mum and dad were going to be turned to atoms.

He had sixty seconds.

Chapter Thirty

The Royal Digit

It was not enough. As the Queen's posh voice rang
out of the loudspeakers, as Wagstaffe pushed and
scratched and spat, he knew he was too late.
Bobbing through the multitude, being barged one
way then another, he caught glimpses of the
platform, the men in uniform, the Monarch in
powder blue (with hat, not crown, on head). He
caught glimpses of the sky also (another kind of
blue), and the Floyds Tower, like a Meccano
carbuncle, red, green and ugly, with a whisp of
steam rising from the top. The Queen had moved
from her podium to the electric panel. Above the
button, the Royal Digit dangled, (that's a finger,
pal). Wagstaffe was too late.

At the bottom of the platform steps the Guard
of Honour stood, in scarlet, blue and bearskin,
quite ridiculous. But to one side of them were real
soldiers, ugly men in khaki with fixed bayonets.
There were contingents of marines, as well, and
Royal Navy men, and Air Force – watching him.
As Wagstaffe advanced like a small whirlwind, they
licked their lips and leered. The Queen's last words
– "And now, good subjects, I declare this fountain
well and truly ready to squirt!" – were drowned

from his ears by the clattering of three dozen rifle bolts.

So he jumped. He flicked a switch, and rose above their startled faces like a small gazelle in trousers and a shirt. He landed on his hands and knees, which Her Majesty clearly thought he'd done on purpose, and very proper, too.

"Good gracious me!" she said. "It is one of the Great Unwashed! No need to grovel, animal, one is much too busy for that sort of thing, one has work to do!"

And, every inch the Head of State, she pressed the button with a little gracious smile and stepped back to her podium.

At which instant Wagstaffe disappeared beneath a mountain of uniforms and boots. The military had clobbered him.

Chapter Thirty One

A Pair of Live Wires

The next part of the action lasted – by the stop-watch – precisely two minutes. That was how long, you will remember, the coloured fluids in the Tower would circulate, building up to pressure, before the fountain burst high into the sky. That was how long it would be before Waggie's mum and dad were squeezed and minced and blasted through the hole. That was how long he had to remove twenty-seven soldiers, sailors and airmen from on top of him and Do Something.

Inside the Tower, Willie and Englebert were being thrown about already, like ball-bearings in a pinball machine. Hot water and steam were gushing everywhere, sharp angles were catching at their clothes, trapdoors were clanging open and banging shut. Desperately, they held each other's hands, and tried to smile. At least they did not know what was about to happen.

"I'm sure we'll be all right," said Mrs Gribble-worm, quite bravely. "The Simpsons wouldn't let us down, would they? Not really?"

Her husband felt his false moustache fly off. A jet of bright green water caught him in the eye.

"Of course they wouldn't, darling! After all, we've got their money, haven't we?"

(They had not, that was wishful thinking. How they kicked themselves, secretly, for having placed it in the special duct. They both suspected that the Simpsons, damn them, had already picked it up.)

"Oh Engie!" shrieked Wilhelmina. "Oh Engie! I can't hold on! I'm being sucked away! It's *hot*!"

Things weren't much better for Hugh N'Dell, either. He did not have a mainspring, or Wagstaffe's desperation. He had a headache and he was worried for his ferret. As he tried to force his way through the teeming throng, the throngsters tried to force him back. Some people got quite nasty (thinking he was trying to nick their good view of the Queen, even if they did not have one), and bashed him. What's more, he didn't know where Sackville Street might be.

"Please, sir? Could you let me through?"

Bonk! That was his nose squashed flat.

"Excuse me, madam, do you know where –?"

Smack! That was his ear bent sideways. Hughie, sniffing forlornly, battled on.

Although he did not know it, there were precisely twenty seconds left when he was forced out between two fat female bottoms and projected into Sackville Street like a bar of wet soap. At the moment that he saw the Simpsons they gave a yell of triumph and held their black plastic bag to an opening in the wall. Hugh saw something fly out from the hydrant pipe, and saw them stagger backwards. Then they rushed to the wall again, faces greedy, sack open for more loot. Even a strange, wobbling, excited cry from the crowd did not distract them.

But Hughie did. Without thinking, he ran up behind. As he arrived he tripped over another bag, the overnight bag they had had at the doss-house. He lost his balance, and cannoned into them.

Mrs Simpson, almost without drawing breath, hit him with her loaded handbag once more. This time, Hugh N'Dell went out for good.

And on the platform, Wagstaffe gave his everything for one last mighty effort. One finger on his Emergency Power switch, his tin teeth gritted till they sparked, he tensed all his springs and muscles at the same moment. In every direction, soldiers, sailors, airmen and marines flew across the platform. Before they could regroup Wagstaffe – clothes tattered, blood and oil spattered everywhere – marched stiffly to the electric panel, tore off the top, and seized the two biggest wires he could see.

It Was The Moment. The Two Minutes Were Up. The Floyds Tower was shaking and rumbling, the crowd were going Ooh and Aah, the Famous Gribbleworms were about to appear before them as a Thin Red Mist.

Then Wagstaffe touched the two live wires together.

Chapter Thirty Two

The Big Bang

Wagstaffe Winstanley Watkins Williams – quite simply – disappeared. There was an enormous explosion, a blinding flash, a sharp, disgusting smell of burning – and he was gone. It was just like the Blitz(!).

Everybody else on the platform went at the same time – thrown left and right like rag dolls into the crowd.

Only the Queen remained. As the billows drifted away in the breeze, she emerged from the swirling smoke and dust as if set in concrete. She was gripping the podium with both hands, her shoulders hunched with effort. She was the Queen, she would not be moved, she was British!

But she looked unusual. For a Queen, she looked distinctly odd. She had no hat on any more, and her hair was standing up on end, like frizzy fronds of wire. Her face was black and sooty, with only her eyes staring whitely out of it, a silly smile playing

on her lips. Her clothes, no longer powder blue but grey and black and singed, were all in rags and tatters, flapping round her knees and elbows.

A low, astonished, throbbing *oooooh* went up from the vast multitude as Her Majesty slowly came into view amid the smoke. Then the oooooh deepened, changed, and became more shocked as something else took place. A small garment came fluttering from the sky, up in the sun, and settled softly on the royal bonce. It was a pair of patriotic knickers, red, white and blue, the colour of her flag!

A hundred thousand eyes and more looked upwards to the top of the Floyds Tower, seeking a reason for this astonishing event.

And there – dancing on two columns of coloured water a hundred feet above the square, tumbling and spinning like two ping pong balls at a fairground shooting gallery – were the Famous Gribbleworms.

They were both completely naked.

Chapter Thirty Three

Jailbirds

A Life of Crime (like a toddler's birthday party) always ends in tears. What's more the wages of sin is death, or so they used to say in the jolly good old days. So it turned out that Mr and Mrs Williams, and their son Wagstaffe, and his friend Hugh N'Dell, and even the ferret Danferoo, were pretty damn miserable in their nasty, smelly cell a few days later. They had been tried by the magistrates, and they had been found Very Guilty, and they were waiting to be sentenced. The newpapers reckoned fifteen years in jail would be OK. They had, after all, Humiliated the Queen.

The charges had been many, and rather serious. Helping steal four million pounds, appearing naked on a public fountain, riding a bicycle at sixty miles an hour without lights, and carrying a ferret down a motorway to boot. The chief magistrate had been very fierce.

"It is disgusting," she had said. "It is disgraceful and disgracious and typical of you louty Northern folk. To cover our dear Queen's head with knickers! No punishment could be severe enough for that. Wait in the cells till we think up something suitable."

But how had they got there, you might ask? Why weren't Englebert and Willie minced, as promised? Had Hughie recovered from the bricking of his bonce? And where (for that matter) had Danferoo sprung from?

It's all quite simple, and I'll tell you quickly. Then we'll execute them. We'll call a Public Holiday and have a laugh.

WAGSTAFFE. When he'd caused the explosion, Wagstaffe had fired himself three hundred feet (a hundred metres, nowadays) into the air. He left behind a pair of trainers and a smell of cheese on toast – burnt. Up in the sky he found himself surrounded by thousands and thousands of banknotes, torn and soggy. He head-butted one big bundle of them, still tied, and grabbed it as he fell. He landed in a skip of builders' rubble and passed out. When he came to, he counted the cash. Two hundred thousand. Before he was arrested, he stashed it in his clockwork guts.

THE GRIBBLEWORMS. On the point of being

a criminal, bear that very much in mind, and you'll go far.

But now, the fat policemen have come and dragged our party from the cells. The chief magistrate has put on her black cap, and the reporters have licked their hungry lips and unsheathed their ballpoint pens.

Sentence will be pronounced.

Chapter Thirty Four

The Royal Pardon

But a messenger has appeared! A messenger from the Palace! Not on a big white charger, admittedly, but on a very smart-looking bicycle! A small man, with a runny nose and spots! It's like a miracle, a fairy story! In real life, see, you can get justice after all!

Our heroes (and heroine) clutched the rail around the dock. A deathly hush descended as the small man gave a large white envelope to an usher of the court. All eyes were on it as it was passed rapidly to the chief magistrate. She opened it and read. She smiled, uncertainly. At Willie and Englebert, and Wagstaffe and Hugh and Danferoo.

"Apparently," she said, "the Queen was not upset after all. She thought it was – and I quote – quite a giggle, all things considered." The magistrate's voice got faster. "She thought the sight of ten and twenty pound notes fluttering from the top of the Floyds Tower was sort of educational, and brought a lot of innocent pleasure to her subjects. As did the knockers and the knickers, and wasn't that a funny place for a bloke to have a mole? What's more, she reckons the lot what lost the moolah (and I'm quoting still) was Toffs in any case and wouldn't miss a few old million, would they? You will therefore receive the Royal Pardon. I'm afraid that you can go."

Hugh N'Dell put his hand up.

"Please, Miss," he said. "Wagstaffe nicked my passport. Couldn't you at least do him for that? It's not fair."

Wagstaffe dobbed him one.

Chapter Thirty Five

Reckoning Up

When Wagstaffe had paid off all his parents' debts, the money that he'd stashed away while in the skip was much reduced. He'd tried to keep more, but he was a softy, really. He'd been taken in by his mother's easy tears.

"Send back the Rolls Royce?" she cried. "Oh you heartless, heartless child how could you? The neighbours will take us for common failures again! What will Lady Potter think?"

"Oh all right," he said. "We'll keep the Rolls. But the seventeen TVs have got to go."

"But we need them!" his father said. "Good lord, son, I'm nearly thirty years old! I'm past it! You wouldn't expect me to have to *walk* to a *special room* to see the telly would you?"

"But Dad!"

His father raised his voice and ranted. He pointed out, among other things, that Wagstaffe and N'Dell had wrecked a few of them in their fight. Wagstaffe, for a quiet life, gave in.

He gave in on the carpets, he gave in on the fitted kitchen, he gave in on the heated swimming pool in the back yard, he gave in on the marble entrance hall. In the end, after days of argument, *nothing* went back. He paid for everything. His mum and dad, to celebrate, went down the Dog and Lamppost, borrowing a tenner for their booze.

After counting what was left of his money, Wagstaffe did some heavy thinking. He had enough left to pay back Mandy Badsox, so he selected one of the eight new telephones and called her up in Texas. He got the answering machine, which made him miserable, but he left an urgent message that she should ring. Then, with a very heavy heart, he looked up the number of the hospital and punched the digits. He asked for Mr Aubrey Parkinson, and waited.

"Yes. Parkinson, chief administrator here. Be swift. Time is money."

"This is Wagstaffe Watkins Williams. I believe I owe you twenty-seven thousand pounds. Who should I make the cheque out to?"

There was a sharp intake of breath. Then Aubrey said: "Twenty-seven thousand pounds and thirty pence, to be precise. Another three days, incidentally, and the sum attracts interest at thirty-three per cent. Make it out to me and cross it Personal Account."

"Right," said Wagstaffe. "I'll sort it out with the bank tomorrow and send it round. Now – where is Dr Dhondy? I expect you'll want to give her back her job won't you?"

Aubrey Parkinson laughed so hard that Wagstaffe thought – and hoped – that he might choke. When he had recovered, his voice was quite unsteady.

"Dr Dhondy?" he said. "That hopeless Dr Dhondy? Oh no, sunshine, no chance. Dr Dhondy, you see, is destitute. Broke. Starved, for all I care. She's gone back to India, hasn't she? She's disappeared in Poona, or Calcutta, or Bombay, who knows or cares? Dr Dhondy, my young friend, is nothing any more. Good day."

After he had hung up, Wagstaffe thought some more. Dr Dhondy destitute? Not if he had anything to do with it. He riffled through the pile of cash in front of him. Mandy wouldn't mind, would she? And after that call, Aubrey Parkinson could whistle for his share!

At that moment the doorbell went. It was Hugh N'Dell, his ferret on his shoulder.

"Seriously, Waggie," he said. "What about that blooming passport, mate? I missed the German trip, but one day – you never know – I might need it, mightn't I?"

Wagstaffe brought him in and gave him a Coke. Peanuts for Danferoo.

"I'll tell you what," he said. "I might be needing it. I might have to go abroad myself. To India. How about a hundred quid for it? It'll cost me that much again to get it tidied up, it's an awful mess."

Hugh N'Dell supped Coke and pondered.

"OK," he said. "You're on."

They shook on it.